SEAN M. DOUGLAS

From Storm Clouds Come Angels

Trafford
PUBLISHING

Trafford Publishing edition published 2010

ISBN: 978-1-4269-2763-8

Cover design: Sean M. Douglas

Order this book online at www.trafford.com or email orders@trafford.com
Most Trafford titles are also available at major online book retailers.

Trafford Publishing: Bloomington, Indiana

PRINTED AND BOUND IN THE USA

Our mission is to efficiently provide the world's finest, most
comprehensive book publishing service, enabling every author to
experience success. To find out how to publish your book, your way,
and have it available worldwide, visit us online at www.trafford.com

Trafford rev. 3/18/2010

www.trafford.com
North America & international
toll-free: 1 888 232 4444 (USA & Canada)
phone: 250 383 6864 ♦ fax: 812 355 4082

"Sometimes life is not always about understanding what we know, but knowing that we cannot always understand."

*True strength is inspired
by those who truly care...
Through your caring
I found that strength.
Thank you.*

Acclaim for Sean M. Douglas'
From Storm Clouds Come Angels

"Honest and insightful, a true work from the heart!"

"From Storm Clouds Come Angels deals with the elements of life that truly make us human."

"To understand the nature of man's emotional condition is a gift; to express this understanding is an art."

"Spectacularly honest; the novel's pain brings a beautiful comfort to all those who have ever felt alone."

"Philosophical, yet simple and real; Douglas finds the words to feelings usually only felt."

"Magical and profound, rarely is such honesty revealed in words; an inspirational reflection."

"Rarely may thoughts be so well expressed as true reflections from the heart."

"Intriguing, inspiring, insightful...."

Preface

LIFE is a series of unavoidable moments that forces each of us to lose ourselves in a state of confused reflection. It is this confused place that we feel our problems are the only ones that exist, when no matter how hard we strive to understand the various meanings of our seemingly disordered life, the only thing that we find are more questions. Like a carnivorous cyclone, our minds, like a storm cloud, revolve around a universe that we so delicately have pieced together like a puzzle, only to realize that the picture is never quite complete.

Then, just as suddenly as the storm clouds arise in our minds, we are met by calmness, an acceptance, a knowing that we cannot always understand. We surround ourselves by an ever-changing milieu, skeptical of who and what to trust, but too afraid of being alone not to take a chance.

These writings began as a reflection of the turmoil that life so often offers; expressing the mind through written words is often more cathartic than trying to express thoughts through conversation. These thoughts, intended to be a snapshot of a moment, is a wandering of words intended both for myself and for anyone who feels encouraged enough to read them.

Words are powerful and may harm or heal, they may demand sympathy or instil guilt, and they may unlock a hidden emotion or change a way of being, but ultimately words convey a moment in time and a place in history when often the best way to communicate a feeling is through written thought. Words reveal a place within one's self that at times seems so wrong and at other times so right, yet always a mystery of what was and is.

Life is a time and a place that together create a moment. A memory, a feeling, a sensation; it all equates to a single concept of who we are. We often find ourselves lost in a state of emotional confusion, only to find that in the end we feel that we are either better off or worse off, but either way we always are.

Trying to understand these ideas, these feelings and these beliefs often leads us to question what it is that we are doing in this moment and at this place, and whether what we have become is justified by who we want to be.   We attempt to dictate who we are by trying to understand what we are, but we realize that the only thing that we understand is that we know less than we thought and we will never know what we feel. What we do understand is that our lives are an interconnected weave of the people and experiences that we encounter on every plane. Some we love, some we resent, some we admire, some we repent; there are those whom we cherish and those who give joy, those who we lose and those who annoy; we meet people who give and people who take, people who are real and those who are fake; we find passion in some and we cherish them dear, then there are those people whom we look at with fear; yet all of these people give meaning through strife, but it is all of these people who make up our life.

The more my words wander, the more I appreciated – that while one's own problems are always the worst – my problems are no different than the most cheerful spirit or disenfranchised soul. No one does not experience moments in life that are beyond what one feels may be comprehended at any given time or place; we all face moments when we are alone to dwell with our minds, and it is our minds that often take terrible revenge.

This was initially written in desperation, clawing at something that I yearned for, yet in the end I still question what it was that I was hoping to achieve. Looking in one direction I would find my feelings lost in a horizon that stretched beyond the limits of an eternal moon with no scope of comprehension.

These words are written with the honesty of what many minds feel at moments, and despite all its rants and garbled philosophical metaphors that truly have little reason, I have only come to a greater understanding of that which I do not nor ever will know; "It is a tale told by an idiot, full of sound and fury, signifying nothing."

With hope these words will touch the minds and hearts of those who read them simply because they are ideas that we can all relate to. At some point throughout our lives we all share common experiences that despite their pain or pleasure are something that we all feel; it is what connects us as humans.

Part One

I

I recall walking that warm August day. I remember smiling to you, and while you did not so much as acknowledge my gesture, still thinking that it is simple to be kind to people whom one cares nothing about. What made me turn towards you and wonder? Why did you so inconspicuously capture my attention? Funny to think that it would have been just as simple to continue on my way and have you become, like the countless other faces in a day, just another blur in my quest for existence. I suppose something in my heart or mind – or both – was missing, though what perhaps I will never know. Ironically enough, it is what I unconsciously must have assumed was lacking that created a true void as a result.

Lost in thoughts, stolen by silence, words suggest that which I can only understand enough to merely define; the rest may be felt, but never known. I feel a great absence lingering when my selfishness reaches such a turmoil that I tire fast of old company, my restlessness often wrought by the monotony of those I choose to value, and it is those whom I never tire of that I fear I may lose.

My mind gets the best of me, and indeed I know this, yet still I give in. I so often ask myself, why you, before I remember that the questions are why us and why me?

Even the strongest hearts and minds fall to pieces when challenged by the enigma of emotions and the triviality of thoughts; I suppose that it is these moments when I know who to value most. Even in my quietest moments my thoughts echo with questions, concerns, paranoid delusions and whether there is a way to understand the ideas that derive from some unfathomable void.

I have found that people are most comfortable when they are acting a part of themselves that they otherwise must hide. When did reality become only true through deception? Then again can I truly be deceptive if I know that I can never hide from myself? A fact remains, however; true individuation and enlightenment – while offering immense gain – comes at a great cost. Alas, too much confusion.

* * *

Standing atop the 4000 foot apex of Kaala Peak and looking down at the rainforest spread out like a lush green canopy meeting the clear turquoise-blue ocean, I found solitude; I was lost in unconscious thought, in awe and overwhelmed. There I experienced what could be considered a perfect moment, in as much as we can understand perfection to be. I was completely alone yet I felt apart of something so much greater. I missed not the drone of people, the sites of a concrete paradise, the randomness of routine, the hypocrisy that commands respect, the ignorance that dominates me and everyone else. It is not as if I ignore the reality of the world around me, but in those rare moments, something changes which allows us to become a part of a unified whole.

The trees, the ocean, the birds, the sky; they are no longer separate things that I was experiencing, rather they become one, and I apart of it. These moments in life are rare and far between, and I assume moments that many never face; I suppose that despite my openness to appreciating myself and the world around me, the desire to appreciate is not always a prequel to doing so. To not take our lives and nature for granted is very difficult in a global culture that thrives on the concept of necessary consumption.

Everyday I rush past the beggars, I feast on fine foods, and I pull nature from its foundation. I ungratefully wake up knowing that my duty is to exist; I often forget to live. I wake up each morning, not always because I want to, but more because I must.

"Arise, mind and body, today is another day of routine; today is another day of asking myself why". I enjoy what I do; I just often do not want to do it. So why do I and you and so many others put ourselves through this temporarily unending routine paralyzed by duty, dictated by the commonality of what we as a part of the masses have come to accept as the way rather than a way?

Of course I must ask, "Who am I of all people to question what is accepted?" I am merely a simple mind and a simple heart who feels exploited by the tabernacle of society, but even if I wanted to change the way I exist, what could I do and where could I go?

When I was young and knew everything, I wanted to believe that music was the universal language, but alas, I found that melody and lyrics merely reflect the thoughts, feelings and emotions of the individual who composed them and what they felt at that time is surely not what was being felt universally at any one time.

Then while studying philosophy, I constantly came to believe that perhaps mathematics is the universal language. For such an apparently logical system, I never understood the practicality of it; things are only mathematically constant because we have yet to find the variables to change the formulas that are deemed absolute. I once read that mathematics crosses the boundaries of race, religion, sex, creed and so forth; the irony is that so few people understand it. Mathematics, I soon discovered was a contradiction of itself caught between theory and fact only to be found false as it pertained to another theory. Of course perhaps my ignorance towards mathematics feeds my cynicism and perhaps mathematics is an absolute and universal idea that we simply do not understand. The fact remains, however, that as long as we know that we will never comprehend the vastness of the universe, there is nothing absolute, hence mathematics itself cannot be considered an absolute idea.

While mathematics is suggested to rest with the ideologies of science, the natural sciences exists within our understanding of time and space, whereas our understanding of the idea of mathematics does not rest in a conventional plane of comprehension. Mathematics is an abstract form of logic based on the fundamentals of what we suggest we understand, but the mathematical reality is that if we accept the notion of a metric expansion of the universe then we have to accept that all the mathematical certainties that we understand have the potential to change as well. The one thing that we can suggest with great certainty is that change is all we can be certain of; thus mathematics is far from final and hence not something that may be considered a universal truth.

It was after that idea that led me to wonder if perhaps a smile is the only universal language necessary. I still value this idea even though I have found that often it is something selfish that induces a smile, and that those who once would share a smile so readily, have become weary of what a smile may suggest. A smile still seems so simple, so easy, so human; this may be why it is so often overlooked.

II

SO few places are there for me to run and hide; then I think of you and remember all the good that can be found in life. But still, it is never enough. I want to spend more time in your company, share more words of insight and unawkward silences, look into your eyes and see that glimmer of life that so honestly reflects the feelings that you try and hide. These are the moments of life that should be cherished and yet it is these same moments that we often take for granted or put off for another day.

Why do we exist? I mean really, why do we exist? It is not for the sake of obtaining more money or wisdom or love or possessions, and it can hardly be for the sake of others or even our selves. Some feel our responsibility is to populate the earth; I think our duty should be to stop. Others believe we are placed here to simply share ourselves and all the good we have to offer, but quite frankly that is a fairly naive idea, for there is truly no such thing as an unselfish act; no matter what course of action one takes, the act is done with the intention – perhaps unconsciously – of bringing about some form of personal gain.

So often this is argued simply because no one wants to admit that even a kind gesture is an act of selfishness. What is more peculiar is that this idea really bothers people. What is wrong about doing something that benefits others as well as us? We share ourselves with others because we feel good by doing so, but perhaps we fail to remember that someone is using us for similar reasons for their benefit. Every relationship, whether friend or foe, is what it is because each side receives something they feel they need – companionship, conversation, passion, love, spite, money, sex, inspiration, worth, competition; the list is endless.

Great minds lead to great sorrow, though hardly a great mind is mine. I sit all day, everyday lost in thought, and even the good thoughts seem unjustified by how I think I should feel. I think I am a content person, though I often do not feel that way. Trapped in the cycle of despair that has become the way of my world, I find it difficult to escape the continual drone of desperation that echoes from everywhere I turn; a loss of meaning is so evident in my tormented mind. Life, love, nature; it all seems so void of the things that I use to think were important. Frustration dictates my mood, confusion is my result. Anguish becomes a norm, and as the days pass, all I see is the desensitization of what was not so long ago good.

I think of you and appreciate that what we had was something that is so rare to find. Many think they find it, but often they are only deceiving themselves into thinking they have something for the sake of wanting it. Perhaps I too am deceiving myself into thinking I have something more than what I can truly be offered, but you offered me trust, and trust is something that is either known or not. Or perhaps trust is something we want to think we can have, when often we never do. Trust is best described as an emotion that you feel, that you know, and like any emotion, trust can strengthen or diminish with time just as emotion may also be mistrusted and changed.

Why is it that what we fear is often what is truest in our hearts? We avoid what tempts us; we deny what feels good. We reserve our feelings because we distrust what they say. Our nature has been overshadowed by our own hypocrisy. Facing the world with all of our arrogance, we question why nature has gone astray. The disease of technology that we have created out of our desire for convenience has led to an artificial intelligence with the capability of eradicating our appreciation for the power of our designs, thus breaking down our moral conscious to a level of animosity, approaching what Hobbes would suggest to be as our natural state of war.

We have reached an era when Machiavellian[i] philosophies have become the unconsciously accepted regime, where fear dominates compassion and our intrinsic desire for respect has become a product of greed only exerted when something may possibly be gained. We look to our Books[ii] for guidance and help, only to have our leaders[iii] advocate the hypocrisy that we search to overcome.

We sympathize with others simply because it allows us to feel fulfilled, another action that our form of greed takes. Perhaps we should not sympathize; perhaps to sympathy is to accept that the one whom we sympathize for has merely chosen not to use their conscious abilities to overcome their issues. Empathy, therefore, is what we lack; empathy is what we necessarily have to feel to know that our sympathy is real, to know that the pain of another may be experienced within ourselves. But alas, our modern era has us trusting ourselves so little, that to empathize would be to encourage the fears that we would rather not understand, and of course we fear what we do not understand. From a lack of understanding comes ignorance, and it is out of ignorance that intolerance, miscommunication, indifference, misjudgement, injustice, uncertainty and a mistrust in differences becomes a leading basis for thought, to name but a few.

We seek trust in others simply because we do not know how to trust ourselves; we do not want to trust ourselves for we are unsure of what we may find. Then again, if we do not seek trust in others, than we only trust ourselves which will coerce our minds into a constant state of suspicion and allow for no peace of mind, body, and soul. Plagued by how we define the concept of trust, we find that trust is a subjective matter that conveys a different meaning for everyone and everything we know. Great differences may be seen between being honest and telling the truth; being honest may easily be done while forever living a lie.

As a character trait we find trust so integral to whom we desire to associate ourselves with, yet we find discomfort in those whom we should. The honest lawyer and faithful politician have become oxymoronic ideas, creations of a culture lost between its own ignorance of what is wanted in a person of authority and what one in actuality is.

Maybe it is atop of Kaala Peak that I belong.

III

CARPE diem" – Seize the day. Interestingly enough, the words that follow are known to few. "Carpe diem, quam minimum credula postero", or "Seize the day, put no trust in tomorrow". So often, rather than seizing the day, I look in the mirror and wonder, why? I am not vain, so why do I look in the mirror in the first place? Who do I seek to impress? Or is it an impression that I look to discover rather than create? Then there are those days and occasionally weeks when I look not in the mirror, unconscious that I ever avoid looking at myself to begin with. Nonetheless, we so often avoid seizing the day and instead take for granted a moment.

In a culture so immersed in the physical and the superficiality that invades everything that we are and everything that we create, I wonder if such a thing as a free mind is even a possibility. Longing to belong while still striving to be myself, the constant battle that everyone pursues between self and society rages on. We seek trust though we run when we find it; we fear each other knowing that we can take away the strength that overshadows any thought of rationality as we give into each other, yearning for an understanding that we are safe to feel, safe to understand, safe to belong, even if only for a few brief moments. Lost in a welcomed confusion, abandoned by my mind, I embrace those moments – those near perfect moments – when our minds join as one.

Yearning to see, I close my eyes and allow my mind's eye to offer me its unconscious insight into what I perhaps know but fear to admit. Yet, why fear anything? Of course we fear that which we do not understand, but should we really fear what is not understood? Should we not take comfort in the adventure, the mystery, the excitement of the unknown?

Knowledge some suggest is power, but what power exists if we cannot understand the unbridled contempt of nature's loves, lusts and desires, and what good would power bring to a soul as lost in contemplation as mine, given to the mercy of that which I do not know yet still undauntingly seek to understand. Then I look at you and at the world around me and wonder how I can justify searching for meaning when there is one thing I do know, one thing I can trust; myself. Only when one trusts their self is there a lack of immorality, of mistrust, guilt, confusion and greed when the logicality of what I am suppose to think takes over what I know I feel.

So there I sat and there you were and from a distance of worlds apart, a connection was made; eyes speak more passion than words could ever hope to express. It is in those brief moments of the most simplistic of pleasures that we truly learn the most honest lessons of whom we are and the risks we are willing to take to fulfill a fleeting moment in our short lives. For so long I watched in the distance as you passed by like a storm cloud, so full of life, so full of fury, so full of passion and pain. And for such a time, such a long, long time, I waited and I watched feeling the torment of longing and fear, until finally the desire reached such a point that even if I were to lose all dignity, all pride, and all that represents myself and all that I felt so strongly for, my existence would be settled by a simple hello.

We face moments in life when we contemplate a situation; dare I break the silence, should I speak the truth, what if I defy all reason and risk humiliation? But then those moments pass, and usually we think nothing more of them, but there are those other moments that we allow to dwell on our actions while we truly ask ourselves, what if? If there is a moment of limbo in life, it is that second when we ask, "what if". Never should we regret a moment, for never can we change the past. Time passed is lessons learned, and all that we may gain in life is the knowing that we had a chance to experience a time and a place that no other person could ever be in or at. Never should we see a moment and walk away out of fear, out of self-pity, out of the consideration that the same moment may not be followed by another. A true moment is only captured by one who will seize a moment to its utmost extreme at the sacrifice of all that is oneself and at the risk of changing the path of what life meant at the moment before.

So often we stand back looking at a situation, contemplating the risks associated with every variable until the situation is passed and we feel that since we were unable to make a decision, the decision was made for us. A reality is that we cower from what we know we want, from the choices we feel should be made, from those moments that for an instant could bring a new and profound outlook on life and to how we regard ourselves and our relationships with others. From storm clouds brew a fury, a ferocity that is unbridled, an anger that even the gods can hardly restrain; but from storm clouds come angles; and from storm clouds come raindrops that explode with such intensity as they hit the ground, as do those rare moments when we resist our usual restraints only to run out on the street in the driving downpour, look to the sky and allow the tears of heaven to pour down upon us with such vigour that the connection of our own tears get lost in the torrent of those from heaven.

Where do we fail ourselves? What moments take us from a paradise of innocence to a world of moral contemplation where we feel that even honesty is something to distrust? So often we stand in a place and a time and look beyond ourselves to a world not so far away; we wonder rather than act; we stare at a vision in our mind trying to balance where we are and where we could be; we part a path not taken simply because reason told us no; forever we will ask ourselves why.

Seize a moment, cherish a day, and if nothing else, live only because you are here expected to exist. Realize a time when at another place you would run; face another time at the risk of yourself. If there were moments in the past when you would expectedly turn away, face your greatest foe – yourself – and stay.

I have been taught something great, the value of self trust. I have been taught to be bold, brave, and trust what

Sean M. Douglas

I *feel* rather than what I am told I should know. For so long I have relied on reason, on the philosophical basis of rationality, but I taught myself to take all that I know and all that I thought I could confirm and continually convert myself into the person I want to be. I have taught myself the basis of trust, the loyalty of understanding, and the honesty of love. Through love we are enabled to recreate the Trinity in our own ways; first with the mind, then with the body, and finally through the soul. It is in this way that one can create a world where few dare venture, though many often dream.

I often look forward to moments that I sometimes feel I should repent; I drown my thoughts in my sorrows when often a smile would be much easier. I am openly honest in opinion despite other's disposition against truths; I take great comfort being around people, but rarely do I want to know them. I would never cheat, but I will often change the rules of a game. I am proud of who I am and take comfort in my pride. I am who I am and I am real; and so are you.

* * *

The absurdity of the mind is truly a work of art. As I fill my canvas with my thoughts, feelings, ideas, beliefs and reflections, I look to only see more unfilled space begging a brush to bring meaning to an emptiness that some may label as a void. But a void is merely a space still waiting for a thought, for something may not come from nothing unless nothing is something from the start, an argument that alone causes me much unrest as I can only look then to a beginning.

Like our love, evolution must have had some beginning, something where the most basic, yet fundamental foundation of our existence transpired to gradually create the intertwined connectedness of who you are, what I am, and how we somehow are connected together.

What brought us to this point in space and time that we so idly ignore? Often I wonder if paths cross as if a hand of destiny brought them together, but then of course I curse the thought, for never would I want to feel that the control that I suggest to impart upon myself is really the control that is as deceptive as our lives truly are. People beg for mercy, pray for time, pervert their space, and in the process destroy their mind.

We make life more complicated simply by spending our time asking questions that rarely will we find any answers to, or the answers we find will hardly suit that which we are searching for all along. We follow evidence only so long as it defends the answer we initially seek, for as a product of our culture we are persecuted for being unconventional. Memorization is how we justify intelligence, creativity, uniqueness and insight; a difference of opinion is often annulled when they do not compare to the stereotypical ideas of what is deemed right or wrong. Even objectivity is a subjective concept that may only be conceived by means of a bias.

Perhaps I am being too hard on myself, on you, on us as a whole?

IV

SITTING alone, at a place I rather not be at, surrounded by the nature of others that has no bearing on how I feel, I think of you and the joy that arises from the simplest of gestures. So often I would watch you waiting to catch a glimpse of you in a natural state of being; what a smile it would bring to me.

The weather, so frosty, does little to fend off my solitude, for you whom I desire so much to be with are now time and space away. I count the days awaiting to be in your presence, though how many days I know not; your absence feeds a fire deep within me, for every moment of your absence demands a moment of memory.

How can time heal the wounds of the heart when what was had is too cherished and too profound to ever want healed? I yearn to touch your hand, to feel you close beside me; I have relearned that life centres not on all the melancholy of the entirety of life, but in those brief moments that are so good. I can almost picture my own face wincing in painful thought; I miss you.

Not a song plays over, not a face passes by, not a book or a piece of art do I see that somehow does not trigger a memory of a moment so long past but more vivid than forgotten. Through weakness and strength, little defends even the surest mind from the relentlessness of the heart that so easily comes in its many forms.

The imprints that we leave on life are so unconscious, so unnoticed, yet so real. Many times have I watched my footprints in the sand so gently be washed away by the warm sea; do our prints still exist as a constant of a past space and time? I still recall them in my mind, thus they must exist. You also are distant, though the imprint you have left me with is hardly washed away and far from being forgotten, though I am faced with the struggle of understanding the deception of reality.

Why chose to promote the specificity of life when life is a deceptive reality to begin with? Nature, for instance, is all that we are and all that we will be, and yet nature itself is an idea that exists within a realm that we can hardly fathom. Nature and God are equal; both perfections that have been created merely out of that which one cannot know to exist. So why formalize one's self to these deceptions and structures of deception founded on the theories of questions we do not even know how to ask? As destructive creatures of habit, we maintain anticipated and expected formulas of survival, only ever accomplishing what is essential rather than what is desired.

But what is it that we truly desire? Can one really desire anything beyond what one believes can actually be achieved? To desire is to strive for what one wishes to achieve, yet few ever endeavour upon achieving that which is most desired. Perhaps the solution is not to desire, but of course how can I even pretend something so absurd. I look at you and want nothing more than the simplest of pleasures.

To renounce one's desires is to renounce what makes us human. Can one actually renounce desires without achieving death? Or maybe death itself may be something to be desired. Can one revoke humanism and enter into a true state of nature, or is that simply suggesting that once man enters a state of nature, that state of nature will become humanized? Perhaps, but not necessarily, for man is a part of the state of nature. But humanistic greed is such that we cannot simply be content with nature in its natural state; we must taint nature with everything we are until what remains is a memory of what we once desired. Have you and I tainted what we once so desired to the point where we now question what we knew to be so real and so good as a product of passing lust? I beg to disagree, for after this much time the notion that a passing lust could still feel this strong can hardly be a lust worth letting go.

We punish ourselves for that which we know we want, though once we have that which we so much wanted, we grow bored and bitter and curse ourselves for allowing something so socially unacceptable to have even taken place. I feel no guilt, no wrong and no worries; why would I?

V

PYGMALION[iv] spent his life in torment, seeking his notion of perfection only to realize that perfection may be sought, but never found. Instead, Pygmalion created his idea of what perfection represented; a masterpiece of all that he desired, all that he thought that was good, and everything that he wanted to love. By the grace of the gods his fantastical creation of perfection became a reality, yet still it originated as a product of his mind.

Dare I suggest that I too seek a perfection that I never will find? Or do I desire perfection so much that even if I did find this perfection, I would never see its truth past my own desires? Perfection may only be found as an idea of the mind and cannot – nor perhaps ever should – exist in any form of reality. Even within the mind the notion of what perfection is makes little sense since we have no concept of what makes something perfect. There is nothing so perfect that one could not conceive of some form of change, thus if the possibility of change exists the notion of perfection cannot, suggesting that even our idea of perfection is so imperfect that any proposition of something involving an element of perfection may be accepted as flawed. Alas, people are so perfectly imperfect.

To conceptualize my thoughts is such an interesting task. So many emotions, so many thoughts, so few words, and of course there is always the question of why am I doing such a thing to begin with? Then again, what is this thing I am doing? My thoughts truly are something that is verbally inexpressible, and yet here I sit amid my books and drink still making a lame attempt at communicating the silence that makes up my mind; sharing thoughts is a method of objectifying experience; I like that and find that notion hard to discredit.

Perhaps I am trying to legitimize what I am thinking, justify what I do, acknowledge how I feel, and all in such a way that allows my sanity to remain an element of myself that for now I still maintain.

Something that intrigues me so very much is the notion that we just are, and despite any action, any thought, feeling, opinion, or belief, we are still just what we are. No matter how hard we try and avoid ourselves and no matter whom we fear, we still just are and there is something beautiful and wonderful about that idea. We all have a role specific unto ourselves that draws an aspect of who we are into what we want to become.

We seek a *soul mate*, that perfect partner whom we want nothing more than to share our mind, body, and soul with; but then a strange thing happens, and in the natural course of life, there comes along someone else that is even more perfect then that one whom we thought was *the one*, and our desire to share ourselves with that person shadows everything else prior. Amazingly,   we never truly understand the significance of what our mind, body and soul have had on different people, yet we are forever changing the lives of ourselves and others. By simply being honest with who we are, with what we are, and with the people who we are with, wonderful things occur in ways that we will never understand.

Part Two

V

TODAY is that day. The day one truly fears in one's heart of hearts. I lost her. All the effort, all the love, all the time, and now all I have are fading memories. To find one so equal, so charming, so full of life, thought and love, only to lose that person to a battle that wages over the mind and heart hurts as if little else matters. As I attempt to sit tall with pride and hold back the tears that I shed through selfish suffering, a drop trickles down my cheek as another memory passes. Best friend and compassionate lover, you gave me more than anyone else ever could have, and while of course many people will come and go, what we shared was different and unique.

Now lost in drink, I mourn for our loss and for my lack of understanding. For all the knowledge that life has given me, and for all the wisdom and insight I thought I knew, I now only feel an emptiness that was once overflowing with joy, compassion and sharing. With whom will I share my thoughts, my secrets and my deepest, darkest beliefs? Whoever suggested that time heals old wounds perhaps never truly cared, for there will always be a point in time and space where a memory was written, things were shared, and for that moment that was the only place one wanted to be.

There is something so sublime about the mysteries of the heart; on the one hand I sit here lost, feeling hopeless and useless and cheated, but on the other hand I cannot help but wonder at my own ignorance, at the fact that no matter how hard I try, I will never fully understand. But then the tears spill forth and again my body takes over, flashes of memories come flooding back and again all seems like nothing but a heavenly nightmare; so real, so needed, so desired, but so distant and gone.

From storm clouds come angels. Your words echo like sympathetic daggers as you suggest that distance is the cure to that which not even you can understand. Why is it wrong? How can something so good be so wrong? Caught up in the societal misconceptions of what our culture deems as appropriate, you, the strong-willed master of your domain, have succumbed to what is *right*? What is right? Is not *right* those elements of life that make us laugh, that make us love, that make us yearn for one more moment? Is not *right* the times we value, the lives we touch, the thoughts, feelings, and joys that we share? Is not *right* those moments when all you need is someone to listen, someone to have, someone who you know cares unconditionally and at any place and at any time?

Our culture has become so idealized that we have no concept of what ideals to value. We listen to the media and focus on the death and sorrow that sweeps the world while we turn our backs on the things we know would carry us through even the most horrific of times. We demand convenience at the risk of out health, our happiness, and our values. We demoralize ourselves to such an extent that we are blind to the obvious and oblivious to the truths, swept away by the torrent of hypocrisy that has become the accepted nature of our ways, and completely unsure of ourselves when something comes along that we know is right. We choose wrongly because we fear what others may think; we fear what we may think. We are sceptical towards others, mistrusting to those we trust, and cautious about knowing ourselves. We have become a mechanization of all that we tire of and all that is wrong, cast in moulds that replicate what we have deemed to be better, to be easier. The age is upon us when we have become what we fear most, unreal and inhumane.

From storm clouds come angels, but 'tis the angels who take us away, though what is worse than losing someone to death is losing someone in life. Knowing that you are out there –somewhere – thinking of me, trudging the streets, lost in the monotony of routine all while missing a piece that was so much a part of you nauseates my heart for I am here feeling much the same, but unable to do anything. Time is our worst enemy. Time is the one thing that we can never have back, never take back, never change. Every moment of everyday sets the stage for what will change in time, and so oblivious are we to this that we do not even appreciate the changes we are making. Like a trampled butterfly[v], the affects of what we create in our courses of action will always remain a mystery, but we can look at our present and visit our past and attempt to guess at where it may lead us in the future.

Faced in moments of contemplation, I sit and ask myself, am I happy? Usually I answer yes, but that is not the happiness I mean. I mean am I really being who I want to be? If I could change my position in life, would I want more freedom of mind and body, would I rather be in another place, am I only here and now because this is the routine I am use to and have accepted as a way of life? Have I created a situation where I am responsible for the feelings and actions of others and as a result feel trapped in the totality of my own design? Did I even choose this design? I am here, I must have chosen to be here, in this study, writing these words, feeling the pain I do, but why not stand up, walk away and leave it all behind? Why not? And yet I cannot.

Life is not always so forgiving when we lose something we never wish was lost. I cannot help look at you and feel a sadness at your losses; such hurt, such an absence of those who you once so loved. How can I feel anything but respect for those who must deal with loss? Then I also consider the linear aspect that makes life so valuable; we must face the fact that we are quite finite and respect that while all we are is change, our one certainty is death. The moment we take our first breath is the moment we begin to die, destined to a life of contemplation before the inevitability of life's greatest gift of mystery, life's only and ultimate design, the one end that we all reach despite any choice we ever make.

You, so wonderful, have taken a piece of me when you left, but you are far from gone. Worse than losing someone in death is losing someone in life, yet somehow a decision was made and our love was considered more trivial than then the joy that it brought; in a life of so little time, one often chooses to mourn the loss of living moments rather than praise the moments we may still have.

Sacrifice is something that we make at all moments of life; not a decision may be made without sacrificing alternative actions, but when and how do we justify the sacrifice of life, of love, of the grandness that joy may bring? Then the question may be asked, why the need to make sacrifice at all if the choices we make may be met through compromise? Granted, even compromise involves sacrifice, but is that not what is necessary to enjoy the act of sharing?

There is a place for everything and everything has its place. At any moment in space and time each action, each event, each thing is in its proper space at its proper time, for there is no logicality in suggesting that something is not in its space or time if it is there and then.

The time is now, the place is here,
Let's not be scar'd, let's have no fear.
Two strangers met; something chang'd,
A thorn remov'd, a glance exchang'd.

We question this, our time, our past,
We live a life we cannot last.
And yet you yearn to move ahead,
Without the love, that without you I dread.

Then comes the day that we belong,
In space and time we find no wrong.

Sean M. Douglas

The drummer beats his heart content,
My body us'd, my heart is spent.

Butterflies; love laid to rest,
So much time, we ignore we're bless'd.
A chance refrain'd, a thought occurr'd,
Our time, our space has all been blurr'd.

Then comes the day, that we belong,
In space and time, we find no wrong.
We watch the wind, the stars all shine,
Through space and time we craft design.

For just a time we find our way,
We know each other, memories will stay.
We say farewell, but something's gone,
A time so good has gone so wrong.

VI

CREATIVITY often stems from undesired situations; I have always believed that little creativity comes from happiness. I suppose I take for granted that when I am content I spend little time contemplating on the moments when I am actually at ease – for to do so would only ruin the feeling – but it is in those moments of dark creativity that I am most lost, confused, in a state of sorrow, yet inspired to be my best, and it is those moments when I am inspired by all that I seek to understand; it is those feelings of loss, confusion and sorrow that become my greatest friend. Indeed there is little irony in that.

I often wonder how I can maintain that level of misery without becoming a casualty of my own self. The last thing I want is to become a burden, only craving sympathy, for there is nothing inspiring in that.

You inspired me. You still inspire me. Through your love, through your pain, through all that you fought for and all that you achieved, through all that you lost and the failings you felt; you inspired me through your passion, your individuality, your interest, and your beauty. Like a butterfly's image caught on a canvas, you inspired me by your strength to defy the odds and still return to reality. You inspired me for I was not able to do so much on my own.

There was a time when my ego spoke with little restraint, but now as I reflect, I find I am much more modest, much more humble. Inspired by even those moments that I consciously do not perceive you, somehow my unconscious thoughts of you are filtered through and all I feel is a result of you.

When I look back on the creation of my mind, I find few words to explain where those thoughts came from and how they took the form they did. A sketch, a painting, a song; all inspired. An expression may be revised for eternity, and while there was a time when I would simply not let go, now I find that all I have is myself left with honest thoughts of moments I fear will fade; it is all too easy to express a moment in such a revised form that eventually the moment becomes not the one remembered, but rather a new moment created while the true moment is lost. Alas, that is when our opportunity to inspire and to be inspired fades away.

VII

SO often we look for justification in where we are, what we are doing and why, but why question a moment when for that moment we are in that time and that space and can be no where else at any other instant?

We truly exist caught in a moment; once a moment is past it can no longer exist thus can never be changed, and while we exist in the present, the present becomes a chain of moments each of which cannot be prevented nor altered; while we can conceive of what may occur in a future moment, we will never reach that moment, for once what we conceived as a future moment becomes a present, that chain of moments in an instant becomes part of a past.

I often wonder how one can look back fondly on a past but then question that past when it was all within the time and space that it was in; why regret when nothing can ever change a moment, and when every moment of life is a part of life's whole. How may a true experience ever find solitude in regret? In life all one may achieve is experience, all of which leads to our ultimate outcome. No matter what time we are in and what place we are at, we all obtain the same result; the one thing that we can all be certain of is our own demise. This alone may be a justification for partaking in those moments that we subjectively feel as immoral, soliptic[vi], or simply wrong.

Time is all we have; people are all that we can share that time with.

There are those moments when one is put in a situation that results in a complete loss for meaning. Shock is only a reaction; the feelings that follow are the consequence. And who, but those whom we love, can we run to, talk with, cry to, to express all that is in our hearts with.

We all face our struggles – for that I completely understand – but I can still not comprehend the notion of losing someone in life.

Perhaps it is merely my runaway thoughts and my interpretation is wrong, but the thought of forever losing someone so dear is a feeling I wish not to follow. People become a part of us that we never thought we had; a part of us that we never knew existed. There are those whom become the dearest people in our lives, those whom become the people that we are excited to share our thoughts and experiences with, to tell of the insignificant things that no one else cares about, and those whom we know that we can trust with life and love.

We build relationships that are so strong; I cannot understand why there is often such confusion. Why challenge what we know is good. What is a friendship if it is not based on all that we have built up together? Life now includes each other's relationships, and to turn one's back on it all is to kill a part of who we are.

I understand, yet I do not, and my written words convey little feeling; is it so bad having a person who one can love and trust so unconditionally? Do people get so caught up in the misconceptions of this seemingly arranged life that they fear what they simply do not initially understand? Embrace it, enjoy it, trust it, and trust yourself. Do not take for granted what we each have, for few people will ever experience bonds so strong; to break those bonds is to defy what life is truly about.

* * *

Why are we here? For what purpose do we wake and sleep only to wake and sleep again as if puppets of life's control? If we are here for the sake of money, or work, or merely existing then farewell, but if you believe as I do that we are here to share the brief time that we have been given with the few people in the world that will make a difference, than spend some time and think some more; these are the thoughts that are worth consideration and the questions that those reflections produce. You are not alone in your struggles, so do not pretend that you have to be. I am here and I am in you and I do not want the questions of life to get in the way of life's questions.

We have come so far and have so far to go, so indeed time is what I will give you, but always remember that time is something we can never get back.

We turn our backs on a good moment for fear of what may transpire to be a bad coming, only to in retrospect wonder what life would have been if we were not so naive to believe that this time and this place could have no other direction. Caught in a stagnant swamp of embittered emotion, we find that the easier answer is to run and coward from that which we fear to face and yet know so comfortably well. How often do we encounter a good thing only to turn around and deny ourselves from partaking in that which could only enlighten our lives that little bit more, for there is no such thing as a wrong place and an improper time.

Few moments in life are given to those who truly open their minds to accepting what others would consider great, and even when those moments are noticed, they are often forgotten as mistakes that happened in a moment of need, a moment of lust, a moment of selfish desire.

Few consider that those moments are perhaps the moments when the mind, body, and soul are most at peace, the most honest, and yet still we choose to negate those chance moments and give into a conscious that is dictated by the mandates of what we have been fed to believe. Our human nature has been driven out by the domination of the global need for a universality, to the extent that we have no concept of what a true person represents; the individual has become deceased in the wave of conformity that even you and I – so free-spirited in our nature – are caught up in, and all for the sake of sacrificing what we feel at the expense of ourselves to an invisible field of self-deception that now rests at such a consciously unconscious state that we have no notion of who we are and what we desire to be.

I feel, yet I fear; I know though I neglect; I love, though I attempt to excuse my emotion for a lust of something that must naturally be lacking in my life. And if indeed something is lacking, then why fear it and dissuade myself from pursuing that which would enliven my mind, body, and soul to understand a tiny fragment of the puzzle that I will never fully see?

We live in an ignorant illusion of what we resent, of what we no longer wish to justify; we resent what we cannot justify and we justify what we resent certain that we are unsure of what we feel. The solidarity of a mad mind comforts me to some degree, for while somehow blessed with the gift of thought, my mind has become my greatest curse.

'Tis indeed a mad world.

* * *

I wish no one the contemplation that I seem so often to be plagued with at an ever increasing pace.

From storm clouds come angels, and from my mind comes this curse. Like a voice without control, I forget what a still mind is like, or if ever it was. No switch, no control, I wake to the constant babble that is so profound and frightening and real, looking for something to distract the restlessness of my mind so overwhelmed with wonder that all it wants to do is forget.

Do we all face this battle?

I must assume most do not for I hear the ignorance that makes a mockery of the same things that I label as a curse.

"Wake up".

"I am awake."

"Then fall asleep."

"I cannot. I want to."

"If you want to then let yourself drift off."

"If you would stop your constant badgering I would."

"I am only conscious of the fact that I cannot stop thinking because you keep thinking about the fact that I am so conscious of it."

"This is going no where. Let us have a drink."

Sleep comes less frequently as even in my most exhausted moments my thoughts do not let me rest. I am haunted by the voices in my head, though it is not voices in a literal sense, but more like ceaseless whisperings with so many seemingly random thoughts that I can rarely take a firm hold on any single thought; writing becomes my method of focus, my means of thinking in a fashion that allows me to see what I cannot clearly conceptualize in my mind.

Time keeps passing, though my mind, body, and soul find no relief. Absence makes a heart grow fonder only through despair. Staring at the sunrise – once again sleep did not come – part of me wants to simply be content with being alive, with the fact that I am here and I am now, and that in many ways nothing else matters. We plan for a future never sure if we will see a tomorrow; when tomorrow comes we pity ourselves for not enjoying yesterday as much as we wanted to. We talk about life and what we hope and dream of achieving, but rarely do we take action on our words. Tomorrow will most likely come, yet again we will consider all that we had wished to do yesterday and plan on doing them at another time.

VIII

WHAT about love? What about hate? What about joy and pain? Is it even possible to put those things in the perspective of another time, another space, or do we merely allow ourselves to ignore what we feel, disregard our senses, and pity ourselves because we again fear the emotions we so rarely understand? Yet while we spend our lives searching for what we cannot truly understand, every so often there are moments that we do not need to understand because we know; it is these moments that we have to capture and embrace, for it is them that we will never want to question.

Often we pass up what we know because we are so caught up in the struggle to understand.

We base our lives on loss for that is often what we notice first.

We collect material possessions as a means to satisfying our mental appetite, until we reach a climax where what we have no longer matters as it was only the acquisition of these things that gave us value.

We treasure status and disregard the welfare of ourselves and others.

We feed our egos only to find that somewhere we forgot who we were and are.

We take pride in competition, knowing that as a battle someone else will fail.

Somewhere a baby is born, somewhere a person is dying; right now a new love is forming while another is slipping away, and here many of us are teasing away a love that has not failed, yet has been vested by fear.

Somewhere two men sit on the frontlines of someone else's war, looking at each other from afar – two strangers destined to destroy each other – for a cause not their own and in the name of something they will never fully comprehend.

From storm clouds come angels and from a fog comes some sense of understanding, but of what? Perhaps it does not matter.

* * *

Seems that despite all that we think we want to be, we are never quite content with whom we are. When we realize that we have reached a new intellectual plateau, we find that we only have more questions; when we find a person that gives us everything we thought we could want, we realize someone else could offer more; when we think that we have faced our greatest challenge, we finish with a new feat in mind.

Life is a game of seduction, and you – my wonderful – were one of the greatest things that could have happened. What you offered was not seduction, but heart; not a body, but a mind; not a future, but a moment. As individuals we are constantly striving to better who we are, to have more than we did, to understand more than we do, but occasionally there comes a time and a place when what *is* could not be any greater; it is those moments that allow us to put life in perspective.

People often suggest that we always want what we cannot have, and when we receive what we want, we realize it was never really what we thought we needed that would give us that sense of being satisfied; our wants far exceed our needs, but our wants often become so great that they in actuality become needs. So what happens when something becomes a need to the extent that we are willing to sacrifice our wants for the sole objective of striving to achieve that which we know we wanted and now need? That is when we face a dilemma of the mind and heart that is unsurpassed by anything else, but it is through these times of sacrifice that we find what we truly love. From storm clouds come angels, and through sacrifice comes understanding.

* * *

A wise mind will discover that the only thing one should understand in life is that there is nothing that anyone can understand[vii]; a wise mind I evidently am not. Searching for meaning only leads to more questions that allow us to respect – though not necessarily accept – what is and who we are.

I look at you and all the questions fade, there is just knowing, and yet you fight it; you rather be taken away by the wave of conformity when I know your mind and body speak of the passions you feel as an individual. Like a canvas of your inner self, your body shares the thoughts that only you need to know; yet you fight it, terrified of what others might say, of what they might think, of what others might feel. And again I ask, for what reason and for who are we here for?

Can we not follow our minds, bodies, and souls, and be true to ourselves without hurting others? Perhaps not, but does this suggest that there is a reason why we should allow the trivialities of life that we are so prone to obsessing over to pull us away from the few things we are allowed to know?

Perhaps I am not the best person in judgement; in fact I hardly think I am a model of any form of morality, faith, or clear conscious, but what I do believe is that my intentions are honest and good. I believe that I live true to who I am despite not always being obvious in what I am. I conceal much of who I am for the protection of those I love, not for my own selfishness, but because I truly love and appreciate the people who have given me so much that I fear my truths will in the end deter them from seeing the good that I can offer. While I often do seek to expel some of those ideas that I feel, perhaps I refrain from sharing those innermost thoughts and feelings that rest so deep within me because I fear that what I feel will not be understood to even myself. I maintain discipline over my own secrets, not because I do not trust others to keep them – although trust is a gift not easily received – but because I feel they are wonderful moments better left unsaid. My eyes wander and my body roams, but my heart is true and always faithful to those I cherish.

I have loved more than one on any given day, though never have I felt I had to make a choice. I will cherish my thoughts of then, my memories of now, and my moments of tomorrow, for just as from storm clouds come angels, love comes from within.

We spend our entire lives searching for what we cannot understand, but every so often there are moments that we do not have to understand because they are moments that we know; it is these moments that we have to capture, for it is them that we will never question. Too often we pass up what we know because we are too caught up in trying to understand.

I still genuinely believe – or at least want to – that people are good. It is not hypocritical to suggest that one can be honest without always telling the truth, just as there is still more value in a handshake than there is in the written word. We often trust our hearts even when our minds tells us otherwise, and there is something wonderful about going out of one's way to do a favour for someone who will never know a favour was done.

Sometimes life is not always about understanding what we know, but knowing that we cannot always understand.

Perhaps God's got a sick sense of humour. How fantastic that we can conceive of the concept of God yet still ridicule what it represents, despite not knowing whether or not this idea may in fact be a truth, the truth. We hold this image of an omniscient, omnipresent being that is credited with all that we are and all that exists, and while I cannot deny the actual truth of this idea, I have no disposition against suggesting that I have no desire to accept it. I think the greatest satire is being able to respect that a higher being might exist and yet truly have no justification for accepting it.

How can I not look at what I have experienced and what we have experienced and for even a second take for granted what we have learned? Life is truly a journey, and to deny one's self of such an experience would be to decide that time is not worthy of our existence. Often lessons are learned in retrospect, for after time has passed and we are allowed a moment for life to sink in, then do we truly become a part of what once had been. These are also the moments when many place their emotions in fear, anger, guilt, anxiety, desperation and denial. We too often appreciate a moment, only to regret it in the moments after when nothing may be done to change what was, though much may be gained from the moment just past. Regret is the most foolish and insensible emotion; one may change how they feel and the direction they go, but no one may change who they were and where they have been. To regret is to be sorry for a time and a place that one was in and at but can never change; to regret is to challenge a past that is and will always be. What remains is what we were, and even while our perception of what we were changes, the actual time and place will always be the same. Those who regret find themselves in a state of purgatory[viii], lost in what they feel should have been, but unable to escape what was, while desperately trying to change what will be. Those who regret subsequently fear who they realize they are, only to live in denial until a moment occurs when they appreciate that part of who they have become is a direct affect of what they were.

* * *

We lost ourselves in what even we considered a deception of such grandeur that the line between what was, what we wanted, and what could be became less and less obvious as the moments passed; yet every moment strengthened what was, every moment challenged what we wanted, and every moment begged what could be. But something happened, something so unforeseen that had enough power to shake the foundation of what was, what we wanted, and what could have become. That something is the power that lies behind the existence of everything, the power of ideas.

Consider for a moment a perfect idea. Now consider your opinion of the idea that you believe to be the conception of perfection; is the idea perfect anymore? Nonetheless, try and bring that perfect idea into your reality. Interesting, you know not even where to start. You can fathom what would be a perfect situation, a perfect environment, a perfect creation, but you cannot for a moment understand perfection itself.

What if I suggest that nothing is more perfect than an idea? While perhaps somewhat frustrating, is this not a truth? Then again, the truth itself is not an idea that I nor anyone else has any concept of. The truth is decided through subjectivity; after all, objectiveness is merely one's attempt to avoid subjectivity, but of course this is not possible. Everything objective is founded through one's perspective, and a perspective cannot take form without a subjective approach. Where does this leave us?

Think of those things that have the potential to be perfect. God perhaps? Even God, however, is a concept that man has developed, alone suggesting its imperfections. The gods of the Greeks and the Romans are portrayed with humanistic features; the Judaic-Christian God has been anthropomorphized to such a degree that Christians deem His son as he who died for our sins.

So what is an idea? An idea is each fragment of every splinter that we have any conscious or unconscious knowledge of; an idea is the notions that exist even before, during, and after one even realizes there are no ideas. Ideas are one's life source, or energy. "I think, therefore, I am"[ix].

Descartes focuses on this last notion as the foundation of his philosophy suggesting that one must exist if one can conceive of one's own existence, but where do these ideas originate from? *How* can one consider the ideas of one's own existence?

When one senses something through touch – the causes being heat, cold, pain, itch, and pressure – one's body reacts physiologically. Generally, however, people share the same discomforts which are brought upon by these five stimuli, all of which affect the nerves that correspond to one's sensory perceptions of touch.

That said, the suggestion may be made that if the same ideas are innate in all people, then these ideas must have originated prior to birth. Even this notion, however, creates problems. Can the complexity of ideas be as simple as being born with the unconscious yet natural ability to breathe?

It is interesting to consider the fact that there is never a time when one can think of not thinking. The mind is constantly processing information and absorbing its environment, but this would imply that not all ideas are innate. What differentiates innate ideas and post-conceptional ideas is where the topic becomes really complex.

An individual is conceived with the potential to understand one's own life and their environment. One's environment consists of all the elements that affect one's development; the dilemma, however, is that one can never absorb all aspects of their present environment due to the overwhelming number of ideas that any given element of their environment consists of. Take, for instance, a flower. Each element of a flower – its scent, feeling, taste, sound, appearance – creates a multitude of ideas that expand in all directions of time.

While the idea of time may be a human conception, time itself is not. People often perceive time in terms of past, present, and future, but a reality is that time stretches in a far less linear way then we often perceive. Time is not limited by time as man conceives time to be, but time rather stretches in all directions and dimensions infinitely, as we understand the term. This is evident by the fact that the universe has been shown to be constantly expanding. If the universe is expanding into what one may suggest is nothingness – or space – then even within this nothingness must exist a dimension that expansion may take place within. Time is the greatest idea.

So what is this idea of time? This is a tough inquiry, for time envelops many of the incomprehensible ideas that we can conceive. Infinitude, dimensions, past, present, future, and other related ideas, are all conceptions that are indefinable. What can be done, however, is to conceive of ideas that are perceived to be part of the greater idea.

The dilemma people have with infinitude, for instance, is that they try to define the idea with other ideas which contradicts the very essence of infinitude. Many suggest infinitude to be synonymous to everything and nothing. What is often not considered, however, is that nothing is something since nothing cannot exist without something to justify it. In other words, everything and nothing is the same concept.

Humanity is apt to fearing what they do not understand, thus limits are placed on ideas as a way of defining that which is not understood. Time, being the greatest thing not understood, has created the most precarious of all mankind's fears. The only certainty to life is death. Death is merely an insignificant product of time, yet feared as if it is an idea that can be avoided. As a result, mankind has devised calendars, clocks, religion, and other methods of measuring the immeasurable. Why? Because to admit that time is the greatest idea, and ideas of any type cannot be defined, creates the fear in humanity of the unknown.

One must only think of how man has confined time to observe how nonsensically limiting such an idea is. For instance, consider the limitations of past, present, and future. The past cannot be a true concept since it is a moment that can never be reached; the present cannot be a true concept for once the present is thought to be reached it becomes the past which, as stated, also cannot be reached. The future likewise, cannot be a true concept since the future is apparently always ahead of the present, and to assume that one actually reaches the future suggests bringing the future to the present where the present immediately becomes past, which cannot be reached.

While time is one idea that humanity attempts to define, a reality is that everything that one thinks is limited merely by one's attempt to understand. Humankind has always strived to comprehend even that which perhaps is incomprehensible. Simply discussing the nature of ideas makes this point evident. Interestingly enough, it also reveals that humanity is the only species who is not content with the principles of survival.

All species, with the exception of humans, compete solely to survive. Survival of the fittest is crucial for a species to remain strong, healthy, well-balanced, and thriving. Humans choose not to compete for survival, but rather compete to dominate those elements of our existence that have made survival secondary, such as material assets, political supremacy, and military dominance.

These are aspects of human life that have evolved from the competition of survive to the competition to control survival.

So why is it that you and I compete against that which we know while denying what we want for the sake of satisfying the needs and desires of others? Are we that insecure with our choices and that afraid of change that we rather ignore our new vocation at the expense of our minds, bodies, and souls?

You are what you love, not what loves you; such a beautiful idea that takes on so many profound levels; what you love is a reflection of who you are. To look at something that one has so much passion for, is to look at an image of one's self and see that passion reflected back like an image in a lake, somewhat distorted and yet so beautiful that it can hardly be understood while at the same time so well known. Likewise, it matters not what loves us, for even if we are not loved back by that which we love, or are loved by something that we care not for, the feeling that comes through loving something so deeply can be unsurpassed by any other thought, feeling, or sacrifice. By loving something, that something becomes a part of who we are, what we become, and where we are going. We can disregard our passions as lust; we can busy our minds and bodies to dispel the love that we feel, we can discount our emotions as impulses brought upon by a simple need for something that we lack, but who are we betraying but ourselves when all we have in life is change, and the evolution that we cannot avoid we instead take ignorance of.

There are many things that we control in our lives; change however is not a choice. There was a time not so long ago when I knew who I was, what I wanted, and how to achieve it. I now know not who I am, what I want, or how to obtain it. There was a time not so long ago when I knew that my love could never be denied, and then love took a new form and all that I thought I once knew I cannot now understand. Yet so many feel this and do little about it; they go on their ways fulfilling the expectations that they have created for themselves, oblivious to the happiness that they are ignoring; to accept what one knows will bring passion and joy back into life, means accepting that the sacrifices of one's self and others is inevitable.

As we change, we fear what change will bring despite the fact that we have no power over the forces that are. We try and run from change only to find later that it caught up with us and that as a consequence we are now bound by the purgatory[x] that we place upon ourselves as we delve into a consciousness that casts us so easily into a state of suffering.

We spoke of fate once and were unsure where the idea was to go. Fate has such an unfathomable implication that denies any concept of true existentialism in the sense that we have any control over our destiny. Many take comfort in supposing that our journey is already predetermined, as it allows each moment to be justified by the suggestion that every time and place that we exist within was the only place that we could ever be. Interestingly enough, I find it difficult to argue this since as I have suggested before, that there can be no wrong time or place since there is only one time and place that we can be in and at during any given moment. This also suggests that no matter what choice in life one makes, the proper decision will always be made, for it was that choice that brought us to a specific moment.

I recall being told that in time I will come to understand that the choices that we made and the choices that we make will be better understood; time will tell. I find that whether my fate is determined or not, I still have a sense of control – I suppose that is considered free will – that I dictate, and no matter what occurs, I will face the pain, the suffering, and the sacrifices as the only outcome of what I and you and everyone else has chosen. I find it fascinating to think that whether you wish to accept the notion of fate or not, one can hardly deny that we enter a time and place for a reason.

Part III

IX

AS the final curtain begins to fall, I lie awake in my state of purgatory, that lonely place where I feel I am being punished for the mortal sins that always seemed right. The mind is a terrible thing. I can only wonder when the final slumber will take me. I had miles to go before I sleep, but then in an instant the woods so lovely, dark and deep stole me into their depths, swallowing whatever life remained in my mind and body and the soul that I have for so long denied but now yearn to accept. You are gone, a fading yet still vivid memory, that I am cursed and blessed to remember as I drift away to my self-induced state of infinite slumber. Life becomes a chore when the reasons for living seem to disappear, leaving the mind lost in a numbing state of desperation, no where to run and nothing left to consider that seems worth thinking about.

So here I lie in my final moments trying to communicate the last thoughts that seep into my dying mind. I always knew that death was all that one could anticipate in life, but now to face the moment in all its pain and glory, all I can do is wonder. Finally I shall put my mind at rest and commit what may only be considered the most honest act that a person could ever achieve.

Death is so natural that we know not how to perceive it, thus fear and resent what it has come to represent.

We understand death to be the only certainty of life, yet we do not understand it to be something that we should welcome and embrace as perhaps the truest reality of our lives. With death either comes nothing or something, so why is it that we chose to fear? If it is nothing, then we will never know the difference, and if it is something than we should take comfort in knowing there is more than just the life we live. But alas, our feelings and thoughts when faced with such moments of loss are our most honest ones. We hate life for taking away what we love; we hate the one who left for leaving us behind to remember; we feel selfish knowing that we miss another more for our own loss than for what they experienced; we cry knowing that we still had more to share, more to learn, more to experience.

The whole notion of death is such a foolish preoccupation of faith, intellect, emotional anguish and physical strength; death is a sentiment of what is unavoidable. Death is the one thing we can be certain of, and with the feeling of loss that I am not experiencing, I feel death is the next best thing.

I hardly understand why people put so much fear into something that cannot be avoided; death is our one certainty, the one thing we may take comfort in knowing for sure. If nothing else, death is a friend who relieves all the pains that are hardly escapable in a life of such harsh environments.

Why such mystery in this idea? What is so mysterious about this cycle of life that we know so well? Everything has its opposite: Darkness has light, time has space, life has death. Everything has its own justification that makes *it* what *it* is.

You lost so much in life and gave up on so much of the rest; we both shall now be in a place where little else matters, but while you still hurt, in my final absence I will no longer feel pain. You have proven that for all your strength, it was me who reigned as the strong one, and now you will remain in a state of questions that I have renounced from my life.

Despite everything, I still fight a question so difficult to comprehend; do we go through life as the people we want to be, or does who we are change with every situation? As I lie here in my final moments of contemplation, thinking about the times we shared and the memories we created, I always come to the same thought, did it really have to end? Does it really have to end? I often ask myself, what is it that makes someone strong? Is it the person who never backs down from what they know or feel, or is it the person who knows when to walk away, appreciating what was already had and enjoyed? Did I allow myself to become weak and permit my heart to shatter the rationality of my mind, or is weakness those individuals who do not to let the heart trust its own truths? Did I stay true to who I am and refrain from cowering when adversity took control, or was it a lack of insight that turned my passions into plagues?

I feel such pain when seeing people change who they are, not because that is what they feel, but because situations suggest that to do otherwise would be too difficult a challenge. Where is this voice of reason that commands us to throw down our arms and surrender to the cavalcade of safety as if our will is anything but our own? What logic lies in the feelings of guilt, insecurity, and anger that arise solely out of a mistrust of ourselves when indeed it is only ourselves that will remain our truest ally? When will we accept that our loyalty belongs first to our own being, then to those we love, and finally to everyone else? Sacrifice not the temptation to alter our mind, body, and soul for the sake of others, for with every sacrifice there is a loss; learn to love who you are and then you will learn to love others as they will learn to love you back. Life does not happen in a single moment and thus nor does change. Remember who you were, where you came from and how you belong; ask yourself if who you were brought you to where you are, or whether who you are, is a product of something else. Are you truly who you want to be? I thought I was.

It is amazing how heightened my senses have become in these last few moments, as my body strives to feel one more time what it means not to look, but to see; not hear, but to listen; not to touch, but to feel. Part of me rages in anger; did it really have to end this way? Part of me feels only comfort, for never again will I have to experience the pangs of life. I am on the final path that began the day I took my first breath, and for all the years that I could consider as my last thoughts, all I want to remember is you.

There are so few moments when one truly appreciates one's self and the world around, to actually be in the presence of what constitutes life and its connection to everything and everyone; we fail to understand the notion of living for the moment, because we fear that to say such a thing neglects yesterday and tomorrow. We are a product of yesterday and the possibility of tomorrow, thus today we may eagerly say we are. This is hardly an anarchistic idea of one who feels the need to fulfill every good and bad intention conceived before tomorrow befalls, and this is hardly a romantic concept of an existentialist who is so lost in the conception of each moment being the only now, that there is little need to consider a time ahead; this is hardly a justification for allowing time to slip by and exist in a state of inaction, while the moments that do represent our life add little to our personal history. This simply means that we should appreciate every moment that we do exist and find a reason why we should want to live that moment; from storm clouds come angels, and the people we encounter become those angels.

But with this passion of a moment suggested, is there any dignity in death? Even that I do not know. Death represents an end that one cannot avoid, but where is the dignity in dying broken-hearted, full of moments that with my end will be forgotten. What exists within us can exist nowhere else, for when we cease to exist we take all that was good and all that was bad within us away, and bring to a close something that never again will be known, felt, remembered, or forgotten; they will just be gone.

Will I be remembered? Will someone even make the effort to forget about me? I was once asked by a friend to do nothing but remember him, and in return he would do me the same favour. He too is gone now, another part of my life that gave me so much, but asked for so little. How will people remember me? Does it even matter, for there will be no one left to impress, no one else to share with, no one left for me to remember.

Scribbling what I know will be the last words of all that was me, I cannot help but smile feeling that I was mistaken in always assuming that my last thoughts would be profound or leave a lasting impression; instead I feel little of anything and yet tears well up in my eyes. Some deep part of me knows; some deep part of me understands that soon this will be no more. My unconscious begins its last efforts as my thoughts begin to fade. I look around my dark, cozy study one more time, at the things I have collected as mementos to my memories, the memories that will soon be forgotten. All these things I have collected, but all for what; to keep alive something that was always dying, something already dead? Books, music, art, photographs; my precious pictures of you, moments frozen in time, as if somehow by looking at your picture you will come back to me and redeem me from this that I have chosen to end.

So random it all seems to be, but is there anything that can truly be deemed random? Ordo ab Chao[xi] and the logicality of randomness is something that I think is certain when dealing with probability. There is nothing more systematic than what we often conceive of as randomness on all levels, great and small. To be random would suggest that my actions contradict every aspect of what nature is. My words, actions, and feelings are merely generated through some previous, and often, unknown cause.

Pretty in pink, isn't she?

There is no randomness, just somehow meticulously calculated events that could not have occurred without a prior moment of action[xii] consequently triggered by a wave that has been surging since – ah, and therein lays a further dilemma. Ashes to ashes, dust to dust[xiii], from where did this madness begin? As I considered before, something cannot come from nothing, for even nothing must exist, for if the concept of nothing may be considered, than nothing necessarily exists.

You started as an idea, a thorn in my mind waiting to be discovered, until the day when a simple smile blossomed into a love so strong that death itself is all that would quench it. I remember staring at the stars and watching the wind; we shared so much while saying so little. From somewhere came a trust so sure that all caution was thrown to that same wind that so gracefully cut through the darkened sky in the distance. Time stood frozen, yet raced by so fast; each day we tried to steal one more hour, one more minute, one more second, until our one world would again become two and we have to face our separate ways again. There I would watch in wonder as you walked away always too proud to look back; but then you would, and it always seemed like the last time we would ever experience a moment so strong, so perfect. And then it was.

I have repeatedly suggested that to lose someone in life is much more difficult than to lose someone in death, for to lose someone in life suggests that the potential to share more is still present yet never will be. Closure is that moment when all that is felt and all that was shared, all that was and all that could be, and everything that the mind and body feels is expressed. It is when all of the most important words and feelings must be said and shared in so brief a time that all the past and future becomes a single moment of a time and place.

Then there are those moments, like ours that were so good, that ended in such sorrow that closure was never had. I mourn you every minute, reminisce of all we shared; I pity myself for the errors I made, though I praise myself for those joys we knew. I suppose that without closure it is natural to look back and think that there was more we could have said, more we should have done, more we could have felt.

I am as presumptuous as I am dramatic, as foolish as I am hopeful. I feed my mind with knowledge and my knowledge with soul. I seek to understand what I know, but respect that I cannot understand. I look not for a destination, but rather something to achieve only after accomplishing a journey. Love and loss without a fight hardly deserve a chance. I want more time, yet I know that time is all we have and something we can never gain. From storm clouds come angels, and through reason comes hope, but hope can be an unpredictable force.

I have come to an understanding with myself that often I am better off loving the idea of something rather then what the idea itself represents. Seems such an odd thing to admit, but as I sought one final chance and faced my greatest challenge, ready to sacrifice all I had been up to that moment, a calm acceptance came over me and from the storm clouds of my existence, I understood that everything has its reason; no matter what turn of events were to occur, that reason was still the same.

I dare not imply that I accept the philosophy of fatalism[xiv], for to do so would negate any emotion for my actions and also destroy the basis of morality for myself and others. Not only that, but should there be a greater power, whether I suggest this power to be an omniscient and omnipresent being, a form of energy, or even nature in its most powerful form, then the blame for anything seemingly unjust may simply be placed on that rationality.

We exist for such a short time, confined by the limits of our mortality, yet we seem so fearful of questioning our existence that we do little to change it when we realize something is wrong. At most we share ourselves for a hundred years, so short a time when one thinks of the knowledge that may be gained, the sights that may be seen, and the experiences that one may follow. We settle for what is and fail to ask what could be; we find contentment in routine and forget the excitement of change; we seek control over the chaos of emotion and choose what we know over what is still to be learned.

Is it coincidence that so much of we become is chosen by demographics, or is it a decision of convenience? Is it chance that we deny change or simply a fear of what change may become? We watch ourselves, pace in states of monotony, knowing that while we always desire more, we are unsure of taking another step. We attempt to calculate the odds to a formula that does not exist, so certain that if we wait and watch, life will come to us. Then time passes, and find myself asking, why did I not listen to that one last song? Why did I cut that conversation short? Why when the night was all we had did I go home simply because it was late?

We see reflections of ourselves in others and we gauge who we are through them. We are often images of who we associate with, for why would we otherwise associate ourselves with people who we have nothing in common with, whose philosophies and goals contradict our own, whose visions of life are so drastically different that we begin to forget who we are; or perhaps that exactly the point. But what happens when we notice a change? When we know who we once were, but not who we are now? These epiphanies are perhaps the greatest struggles in life, for it is these moments when we need to make a decision, to be, or not to be; to continue on as the person we were, or as the person we have and will become. These are moments when a decision may alter a routine or a lifestyle, but what always must be considered is, what if change is averted and life simply goes on?

I often consider why it is so easy to not want to change, but really the idea is simple; it is much easier to live in a rut, a routine, a consistency, a constant state of habitual control, then to try and change all that we know so well.

We often seem to forget that there are many of us involved in this life, though rarely is it mutual as to when or how a bond will end and rarely are we even offering a warning or opportunity to share any thoughts on the matter.

You once said that in time I would come to understand the reasons why at times sacrifices must be made, and I have. I now understand that for too long I have sacrificed the things that meant the most to me: love, individuality, freedom of mind, passions. Now is my time to face my end in all its cruel and glorious beauty.

Epilogue

AND who am I now that I am gone? I am you. I am all the lonely thoughts, the sentimental feelings, the unconscious struggles that we all face in our lives. Not race, nor creed, nor colour, nor morals make a difference to who I am; who I am is no less different than who you have chosen to be. Not loss of love, loss of life, loss of liberty, joy, health, glory, even pain makes who I am any more or less different than you. We live, breathe and think as one, and the feelings and thoughts that pass before us all are no different. We look for inspiration from others when we feel the need, but all they do is look in the same place that I do and you do. I am the lonely wanderer who ventures the darkened streets in search of answers only to return home with none. I am the tear the run downs your cheek when you are touched by a memory, touched by sadness, touched by joy. I am only what you are and only what you will be. I am what I am[xv] and I am what you are as together we all are as one.

Another time and another place, is here and now.

Endnotes

[1] Respect instilled through fear is a Machiavellian principle suggesting that respect through kindness will only have the consequences of being taken advantage of, thus to promote followers to fear ensures that they will not take advantage of their situation nor have the confidence to make a conscious change.

[2] Throughout history there have been a few select books and thinkers that have become the foundations for man's thoughts, feelings, and beliefs. Of these are such books as *The Old Testament*, *The New Testament*, *The I Ching*, *The Upanishads*, *The Koran*, *The Kabbalah*, Homer's *Iliad* and *The Odyssey*, *The Divine* Comedy, the works of Shakespeare, Keats, Blake, Johnson, *The Encyclopaedia*; such writings from philosophers like Aristotle, Hippocrates, Plato, Socrates, Sartre, Aquinas, Hobbes, Rousseau, Kant, Locke, Descartes, Bacon, Hume, Mill; and such thoughts from great thinkers like Confucius, Martin Luther, Machiavelli, Hitler, Calvin, Copernicus, Galileo, Freud, Nietzsche, Einstein, Hawkins Jung, Buber, and the list as limited as it is goes on. 'Tis these people who have set the stage for how those who follow interpret nature and all that encompasses man as a product of nature; however, the thoughts of one should as a result of natural law spawn the thoughts of another in the form of reflection, scepticism, inquiry, or further insight through acceptance.

[3]Those whom we have always accepted as our leaders – the Clergy, educators, religious leaders, political figures, monarchies and so forth – have become pawns of hypocrisy. They lead their people with a strong hand and an outstretched arm, but they fall prey to their own weaknesses of 'sin' (see sections on the seven deadly sins). One who is human can no more be expected to rule as anything but human with all of the fallibilities that are universal to mankind's nature. The difference between one of power and one of commonality is the number of those whom one may affect through their courses of decision, action or inaction. What begs to be asked, however, is should one of power be rewarded more profitably than one of commonality simply because of their held position? I would suggest that one should be rewarded according to the number of people that one affects seeing as it is what they instill within the minds of many that shape the future of tomorrow whether for a greater good or otherwise. The question, however, is what if the power that one bestows over others is truly an objective concept of what is generally conceived to be good or evil?

[4]The story of Pygmalion and Galatea is a Greek myth that tells the story of a king of Cyprus and his creation Galatea. Seeking a woman to meet his standards of perfection and finding none, Pygmalion created an ivory statue of a woman in its most perfect state. Falling hopelessly in love with his creation, Pygmalion realized that the one element missing in Galatea was the reality of life. Aphrodite, the goddess of love and beauty, saw the genuine love and loss that Pygmalion was feeling and brought life to the statue and gave her the love necessary to love Pygmalion back.

[5]Concept from *The Time Machine* by H.G. Wells. Every event of every moment creates a ripple effect that has

an unknown response to future moments. The theory is that even the movement of a butterfly's wings creates a ripple of such consequence that by quashing even such a small event results in significant consequences. Of course one may argue that if this may the case, then any action's reaction is the consequence and at the moment in that time and space a new *present* is created and the consequences of a past action are immaterial and thus inconsequential.

[6]Solipsism is the philosophy which suggests that only the self exists or may be proven to exist and as such is the only reality. The theory suggests that one may have an extreme preoccupation with and indulgence of one's own feelings and desires. This is a fantastic theory which supposes that one's idea of what reality is, is in fact one's own imagination of reality and that only the self exists. Can one truly comprehend the concept that one's own mind may be the only mind that exists and thus determines everything that one deems reality to be? A compromise to the extremity of this idea is the notion that one's existence is theirs alone but not the determining factor of reality itself. While perhaps an issue in extreme psychological cases, this concept of solipsism is very difficult to give much merit to unless one wishes to accept that all of one's senses are a creation of what one wants to believe reality is. That being said, one need not fear what time or place one is in, for the time and place that one is in and at any given moment is the time and place that one has conceived reality to exist within and, therefore, one can be in no other time and at no other place doing what one is doing at that time or place then there and then.

[7]This is based on the philosophical wisdom that "All one knows is that one can know nothing". This idea has been suggested throughout history: Pyrrho (c.360-c.270 BCE)

suggested that one must first ask one's self what things are and how are they constituted. From there one should ask how one is related to these things. The final idea that one must consider is what one's own opinion of these things are. From there one should deduce that each individual has their own opinion of what something is and how it appears (subjectivism), thus of what something actually is beyond one's own opinion of something, one is completely ignorant of. Since the same thing appears different to everyone based on their own time and space, it is impossible to know what opinion is right; we therefore know nothing.

Immanuel Kant in his *Critique of Pure Reason* (1781) suggested that one can know nothing except the appearance of things based solely on what our senses interpret things to be; judgment, in other words, goes no further than what the senses can detect, so far as the external world is concerned. The true substance or essence of something can hardly be determined by what the senses allow us to know, and despite what science or philosophy may suggest, the true nature of something cannot be known. It is similar to asking someone what 'love' is; not what adjectives one would use to describe how love feels, or the characteristics that often relate to how one thinks they know what love is, but what love actually is. It is like asking for a literal definition of what an emotion feels like.

[8]The notion of purgatory (Lat., "purgare", to make clean, to purify) is one that the Catholic doctrine suggests as a place or condition of temporal punishment for those who, departing this life in God' s grace, are not entirely free from venial faults, or have not fully paid the satisfaction due to their transgressions. Dante's 14th century masterpiece, *The Divina Commedia*, is based on the notions of this purgatory.

[9] "Cogito, ergo sum" or "I think, therefore I am". These words were written by Philosopher Rene Descartes (1596-1650) in *Meditation Two: Concerning the Nature of the Human Mind: That It Is Better Known Than the Body*. This idea represents an intuition of one's own reality since the idea of one's self cannot be separated from the self thus suggesting that one exists. This is such an interesting concept, since for one to consider that they perhaps do not exist is itself implicating one of their own existence. There is no way that one who exists is unable not to consider their own existence, and even hypothesis an end to existence, perhaps through death, is simply establishing that at present existence is.

[10]Italian poet Dante Alighieri (1265-1321) spent much time considering the notion of purgatory in the *Divina Commedia* by using the idea as an allegory of human life. Taken from the Latin *purgare* meaning to purify or cleanse, the Catholic notion of purgatory represents a state of limbo where a soul awaits the judgment of God and man is confined to deal with their sins in a state of suffering before entering the gates of Heaven. Upon entering Hell, however, Dante's inscription on the gates reads: "Through me you enter into the city of woes, Through me you enter into eternal pain, Through me you enter the population of loss. Justice moved me high maker, in power divine, wisdom supreme, love primal. No things were before me not eternal; eternal, I remain. Abandon all hope, you who enter here" (Canto III, lines 1-7).

[11] 'Ordo ab Chao' or 'Order Out of Chaos' is the Masonic motto suggesting that not only is there great order in the world, but it is an order that we as man will never comprehend. The symbolism of the Masonic order is such that it represents the most significant aspects of nature and man in such a way that even the concept of the Masonic

motto casts secrecy upon those who attempt to decipher its meaning.

[12]Newton's 3rd Law of Motion states that for every action there is an equal and opposite reaction. While this, however, applies to motion, can the same be suggested to emotion?

[13]Reference to *Genesis 3:19*. "In the sweat of thy face shalt thou eat bread, till thou return unto the groun; for out of it wast thou taken: for dust thou art, and unto dust shalt thou return."

[14]Fatalism is the philosophy suggesting that each and every event of our individual and collective lives is predetermined by fate. This idea is a very old one that helps one to understand the roles of man and nature and often is a way to justify the malevolent forces at play in the universe. Sophocles (495 BCE-406BCE), the Greek tragedian, felt that there was nothing that one had power over, and that our desires, volitions, choices and so forth were in no way a controlled aspect of individual will. Others, like the Stoics, ancient Greek and Roman Philosophers, felt that the universe has a constant and necessary cycle and thus is unaffected by what we feel is free will; nature, in other words, is an unbreakable chain of cause and effect events that supercedes any individual act.

[15]Ehey asher eyeh: I am what I am.

From Storms Clouds Come Angels: Notable Quotations

"...life is not always about understanding what we know, but knowing that we cannot always understand."

"True strength is inspired by those who truly care."

"We attempt to dictate who we are by trying to understand what we feel..."

"'Tis those whom I never tire of that I fear I may lose."

"People are most themselves when they are acting a part that they otherwise must hide."

"The desire to appreciate is not always a prequel to doing so."

"I wake up each morning not always because I want to but more because I must."

"I enjoy what I do; I just do not want to do it."

"Trust is something that is either known or not."

"We fear that which we do not understand."

"There is truly no such thing as an unselfish act."

"Eyes speak more passion than words could ever hope to express"

"A true moment is only captured by one who will seize a moment to its utmost extreme at the sacrifice of all that is oneself and the risk of changing the path of what life meant at the moment before."

"Realize a time when at another place you would run; face another time at the risk of yourself."

"If there were moments in the past that you would tend to turn away, face your greatest foe, yourself, and stay."

"To desire is to strive for what one wishes to achieve, yet few ever endeavour upon achieving that which is most desired."

"...perfection may be sought, but never be found."

"Perfection may only be found as an idea of the mind..."

"To renounce one's desires is to renounce what makes us human."

"...life centres not on all the melancholy of the entirety of life, but in those brief moments that are so good."

"...sharing thoughts is a method of objectifying experience."

"We all have a role specific unto ourselves that draws an aspect of who we are into what we want to become."

"We are sceptical towards others, mistrusting to those we trust, and cautious about knowing ourselves."

"Time is our worst enemy. Time is the one thing that we can never have back, never take back, never change."

"...all we are is change, our one certainty is death. The moment we take our first breath is the moment we begin to die..."

"...there is no logicality in suggesting that something is not in its space or time if it is there and then."

"Creativity often stems from undesired situations."

"...once a moment is past it can no longer exist thus can never be changed..."

"...why question a moment when for that moment we are in that time and that space and can be nowhere else at any other time?"

"Time is all we have; people are all that we can share that time with."

"Shock is only a reaction; the feelings that follow are the consequence."

"...it is one thing to lose someone in death, it is fully another to lose someone in life."

"The absurdity of the mind is truly a work of art."

"...something may not come out of nothing unless nothing is something from the start..."

"Few moments in life are given to those who truly open their minds, and even when those moments are noticed, they are often forgotten as mistakes that happened in a moment of need, a moment of lust, a moment of selfish desire".

"We live in an ignorant illusion of what we resent..."

"Absence makes a heart grow fonder only through despair."

"...we pass up what we know because we are so caught up in the struggle to understand."

"As individuals we are constantly striving to better who we are, to have more than we did, to understand more than we do..."

"...wants often become so great that they become needs."

"It is simple to be kind to people whom one cares nothing about."

"My duty is to exist; I often forget to live."

"We seek trust in others simply because we do not know how to trust ourselves; we do not want to trust ourselves for we are unsure of what we may find."

"We resent what we cannot justify and we justify what we resent as if we are unsure of what we feel."

"We plan for a future never sure if we will see a tomorrow; when tomorrow comes we pity ourselves for not enjoying yesterday as much as we wanted to."

"Often we pass up what we know because we are so caught up in the struggle to understand."

"...through sacrifice comes understanding."

"Nothing cannot exist without something to justify it."

"Limits are placed on ideas as a way of defining that which is not understood."

"Everything that one thinks is limited merely by one's attempt to understand."

"Humanity is the only species who is not content with the principles of survival."

"You are what you love, not what loves you."

"Life becomes a chore when the reasons for living seem to disappear."

"Death is so natural that we know not how to perceive it, thus fear and resent what it has come to represent."

"Our feelings and thoughts when faced with such moments of loss are our most honest ones."

About the Author

Respected for his profound perspectives on the human condition, Sean M. Douglas spent many years on tour in the amusement industry before receiving degrees in philosophy, religious studies, and English as well as a number of business certificates. As a member of the clergy, he balances life between his passions and his pursuits.